John Smith is NOT BORING!

My name is John Smith – the most boring name in the world. Dad says with a name like John Smith no one will EVER make fun of me. Mum says I'm "one in a MILLION". My sister says it makes me the most boring person in history. But do not judge a book by its cover. My life is ANYTHING but boring!

To Lottie-Lou, Daisy-Doo ... and Florence too!

First published in the UK in 2015 by Scholastic Children's Books
An imprint of Scholastic Ltd
Euston House, 24 Eversholt Street
London, NW1 1DB, UK
Registered office: Westfield Road, Southam, Warwickshire, CV47 0RA
SCHOLASTIC and associated logos are trademarks and/or registered
trademarks of Scholastic Inc.

Text copyright © Johnny Smith, 2015
Illustrations © Laura Ellen Anderson, 2015

The right of Johnny Smith and Laura Ellen Anderson to be identified as the
author and illustrator of this work respectively has been asserted by them.

ISBN 978 1407 15194 6

A CIP catalogue record for this book is available from the British Library.

Printed by CPI Group (UK) Ltd, Croydon, CR0 4YY
Papers used by Scholastic Children's Books are made from wood grown in
sustainable forests.

1 3 5 7 9 10 8 6 4 2

www.scholastic.co.uk

Chapter One

"'Tis I, Cap'n John Smith, the fiercest pirate that ever sailed the seven seas!"

I grab my trusty sword and leap on to the deck of my pirate ship. "What's that, my fine parrot friend sitting on my shoulder? Yes, I quite agree. I AM the most dangerous name in the land..."

I go to work putting my enemies to the sword.

SLASH! PROD! POKE!

"You reckoned without the great John Smith," I roar. "What have you got to say before I send you to the bottom of the deep blue sea?"

"Can I have the cucumber back, please?"

"See how she begs for her cucumber! But I show no mercy. I laugh in the face of such pleading! What's that, my fine parrot friend? You are right! This is not a cucumber but my razor-sharp pirate dagger!"

"It's a cucumber! And that isn't a parrot, it's a tea cosy," shrugs my sister, Hayley. "It belongs on a teapot."

"DO NOT INSULT MY PARROT!"

"And your pirate bandana..."

"You mean the headscarf on my head? What of it?"

"You do know they're a pair of my knickers, don't you?" snorts Hayley. "My

3

dirty knickers?"

"What! Arrrgh!!! Brave Cap'n John Smith, undone by his sister's smelly knickers..."

We gather round the kitchen table and start munching our lunch – me, Mum, Hayley and Granddad. Well, Granddad would be munching his lunch if he hadn't lost his dentures. So he's sucking spaghetti through a straw instead.

"Why are you prancing round with a tea cosy on your shoulder and a cucumber in your hand?" says Dad, wandering into the kitchen.

"I'm just getting into the part," I reply.

"What part?" he asks, taking his seat at the table and picking up the newspaper.

"The useless loser part," says Hayley.

There speaks my big sister, the destroyer of dreams!

"The pirate captain," I reply.

"Why do you want to be a pirate?" says Dad.

"Because Hector's having a pirate party," I reply, "and we're all dressing up. I'm going as a brave, dashing, adventurous pirate..."

"How can you be a dashing pirate," sneers Hayley, "when you're whatsischops, the boy with the most boring name in the world?"

"Can I ask you a question, Dad?"

"As long as it doesn't involve money..." says Dad.

"Why did you call me John Smith?"

Dad pokes his head round the side of the newspaper.

"Ask your mother," says Dad.

"Don't blame me," says Mum. "It wasn't my idea."

"Well, whose idea was it?" I murmur. "One of you must have given me my name!"

Mum and Dad look at each other and shrug.

"You were probably given your name by a computer," chuckles Hayley. "Maybe they scanned your face and the computer gave you the name you deserve."

"Hayley!" says Mum. "Don't listen to her; you're one in a million."

"Too right," says Hayley. "One in a million John Smiths."

There's a knock at the door. Hayley throws her fork on the plate and runs out of the kitchen.

Granddad looks at me and winks.

It's not fair, you know. My big sister gets three middle names – Hayley Mutya Keisha Siobhan Smith – after Mum's favourite pop group at the time Hayley was born.

But I am just plain John Smith.

"One day you'll see," I nod. "Just because I'm John Smith on the outside, it doesn't mean I'm John Smith on the inside. There are big things waiting round the corner for me."

Hayley comes running back into the kitchen.

"Oh my gosh," she shrieks. "I take it all back. Look, John, you're rich, RICH! RICH!"

Hayley drops a leaflet on the table. It's an advert with a made-up customer called John Smith winning a prize raffle for one million pounds. "Oh, my mistake," says Hayley, "maybe you're not rich. I suppose they just wanted a boring, dull, average name to use in the advert…"

I step down from the table, throw my dagger in the salad bowl and toss my pirate headscarf in the dirty laundry. The truth is, my big sister – although I HATE to admit it – is right.

My name isn't exactly exciting, is it?

"I'm going up to my room," I sigh.

"Good luck finding your pirate outfit – Captain John the Boring," laughs Hayley.

She's right about that too. I've got nothing

to wear to Hector's party.

"John..." Granddad hobbles out of his chair, a limp straw filled with spaghetti bolognese in his fingers. "Help me find my dentures, will you?"

Chapter Two

"Where did you last see your dentures, Granddad. . .?"

Granddad moved in with us last year after Granny – well, Granddad says she died, but we know she ran off with a Brazilian dancer called Barry. Since then he's had his own room at the top of the landing.

"Oh, that's easy," says Granddad. "I know exactly where my dentures were the last time I saw them." Granddad looks at me, a smile creeping over his face. "They were in my mouth!"

Granddad throws his head back and giggles, but I'm finding it hard to crack a smile. He stops laughing and sits next to me on the bed.

"What's happened to that happy face?" says Granddad.

"I'll be all right," I sigh.

"I know that," says Granddad. "Just don't let them get you down, OK? You know what big sisters are like. They're devils."

"With you, amigo, a hundred per cent."

Granddad's always full of good advice. It was Granddad who told me NEVER to swallow chewing gum because otherwise you'll blow bubblegum bubbles out of your bottom every time you fart! He is a wise, wise man, my granddad.

"You and me, son, we've got more in

common than you think. We're both called John Smith, for a start," he chortles.

"I know, Granddad," I mumble. "The most boring name in the world."

"There's a little saying down my way," he whispers. "Don't judge a book by its cover."

"Yeah, I think I've heard that saying," I nod.

"See that?" Granddad rolls his sleeve up to the elbow. "See that scar? That's where I was attacked by a sabretooth tiger, and look at this – a flesh wound I acquired as a Roman centurion…"

I start to giggle.

Granddad's always telling me about his adventures, like the time he played frisbee with Saturn's rings or went skinny-dipping with the Loch Ness monster.

"You've got something very special, son,"

says Granddad.

"What's that, Granddad?" I shrug.

"You've got your name."

"Yeah, right," I grunt.

"Trust me," says Granddad. "I know what I'm talking about. Just because you've got

a boring name, it doesn't mean you've got a boring life. You want to go to Hector's party as a pirate, then you have to believe you're a pirate. All the fancy dress in the world doesn't make a difference if you don't believe it in here." Granddad gently taps his chest. "You know what I'm saying?"

"I think so, Granddad," I murmur.

Actually, I haven't got a clue what he's going on about. It all sounds a bit potty to me.

"We'll see, son, we'll see..." winks Granddad.

He slowly gets up off the bed and walks to the door.

"Do me a favour. Take a look under the bed, see if I kicked my dentures there by accident. I would get down there myself, but at my age, I can't be sure I'll ever get back up again."

I get on my knees and stick my head

under the bed.

"You see anything?" says Granddad.

"I can't see your dentures, Granddad..."

"No worries, they'll turn up somewhere," he says. "Wait a minute, what do we have here?"

Granddad suddenly fishes his dentures out of his cardigan pocket. "Here you go," he chortles. "I just hope they didn't eat my toffees!" Granddad pulls a toffee out of his pocket, unwraps it and pops it in his mouth. "You remember what I said..." He smiles.

Granddad skips down the stairs, leaving me sitting alone on his bed.

I fall on my knees and stick my head under Granddad's bed again. Wedged against the wall is an old wooden chest. I close the bedroom door, reach under the bed and slide the chest out. It's big and battered and brown with loads of stickers of faraway places on it.

Inside are hats and capes and swords and wigs and boots and gloves and loads and loads of medals and just about anything you could ever need for dressing up.

I pick out a pirate's sword and eyepatch.

Brilliant. I'm going to be the best-dressed pirate at the party!

I pull on a pirate hat and throw a pirate coat over my shoulders. It's got knobbly silver buttons down the front in the shape of little bendy swords. I do a big twirl and say in my best piratey voice:

"Yo ho ho and a bottle of cherry cola!"

Then I cackle like a real proper sea dog.

Just as I'm closing the trunk, I see something written in old swirly writing on the inside of the lid. I read the words out loud.

"*Say it long, say it loud – I'm John Smith and I'm proud!*"

Suddenly I can hear, what is that ... the sound of the sea? And oh no ... Granddad's room is rolling from side to side ... a salty breeze is blowing in my face, and ... I've just been slapped with a slippery fish!

What's going on?

Chapter Three

"Don't make me throw another pilchard at you, Captain!"

I'm standing at the top of a mast on a really old ship holding a telescope. Seagulls swoop overhead and sharks circle in the water.

SHARKS!!!

SEAGULLS!!!

WATER!!!

When I look around I see that I'm bobbing in the middle of the sea.

THE MIDDLE OF THE SEA!!!

"Well, Captain? Have you spotted 'em yet?"

I see four figures on the deck looking up at me. They are...

A grizzled-looking sea dog with a banana-coloured bandana.

A gnarled old codger with a dagger in his teeth.

A hairy old rogue with a peg leg.
A rascally knave with a fiddle...

And suddenly there's a parrot, sitting on
my shoulder! "*Pirates! Pirates! They be pirates!*"
he squawks.

"Have you seen 'em, Cap'n?" says the
pirate with the banana bandana.

A huge gust of wind fills the sails. The

ship leans right over, almost tipping me into the sea!

"You better come down from the crow's nest, Captain, looks like we got a gale blowin' in," says the pirate with the banana bandana.

So I climb and trip and tumble down the mast, fall through the rigging, lose my footing, crash into a big barrel and come up with a live eel in my mouth, which wriggles free and plops over the side of the ship.

I throw my arms in the air like I meant to do the whole thing and take a big bow.

I think I got away with it.

"Very nice, Captain," says the pirate with the banana bandana.

"Gngnmnphnpm..." says the pirate with the dagger in his teeth.

"What happened?" says the fiddle player. "What was that gigantic splosh?"

That's when I realize the fiddle player is completely blind.

The pirates look like a really mean bunch; they've got scars and tattoos and loads of gaps in their mouths where their teeth should be.

This is incredibly strange. What am I doing here? Maybe I bumped my head on Granddad's bed and stumbled to the party in a daze. Or maybe I'm dreaming. I do get some pretty wild dreams, but they're mainly about giant cheese toasties taking over the world. There's only one way to find out if this is a dream.

I ask the pirates to move a bit closer.

"Will one of you pinch me?" I whisper.

The pirate with the banana bandana looks at me, slugs a gulp from his jug, wipes his mouth with the back of his hand and falls into a rasping, wheezing cackle.

"Nice one, Cap'n." He turns and biffs the pirate with the dagger in his teeth straight in the chops.

"Gnmphphphpng..." says the pirate with the dagger in his teeth.

"He says nice one too," says the blind fiddle player.

Wait a minute. I get it!

This is all part of Hector's party, and instead

of the usual bouncy castle and a pat on the back like I got, his mum and dad have hired him a whole pirate ship and put it in the middle of this great big massive sea with real live sharks! Yeah, that would be Hector all over.

"Well, Captain, you've been up in the crow's nest. Have you seen him yet?" says the pirate with the banana bandana.

I haven't got a clue who they're talking about.

"Do you mean Hector?" I reply.

"I was speakin' of Captain Black," says the pirate with the banana bandana. "He who shall remain nameless…"

"But you just said his name," I reply.

"No I didn't," he growls.

"Yes you did. You said, 'Captain Black – he who shall remain nameless'."

"Do not say the name of Captain Black!" says the pirate with the peg leg. "Oh, blowfish! I've gone and said it now."

This is all very silly.

"Captain Black," says the pirate with the banana bandana, "is the meanest, grizzliest dog that ever sailed the high seas."

"With a wicked temper," scowls the blind fiddle player.

The pirates all nod gravely. They really are very good at the pirate act.

"And he's sailing his ship right for us," says the pirate with the peg leg. "Which is why we're on lookout!"

"Let me take a peek," says the blind fiddle player. He puts the telescope to his eye and points it at the sea. "I can't see nothing at all," he gurgles.

"When I spy Captain Black," says the pirate with the banana bandana, "I'll take my trusty cutlass and do him from ear to ear..."

"And there to there," says the pirate with

the peg leg. "And everywhere in-between."

The four pirates cackle and do high fives – except the pirate with the peg leg, who also has a hooked hand, so he does a high hook instead.

"I like that, Peg Leg Reg," says the pirate with the banana bandana, "from there to there and everywhere in-between."

"*Nice one, nice one...*" squawks the parrot.

"We hate Captain Black," says the blind fiddle player.

"He got the best name in the game!" says Peg Leg Reg.

"And the best beard," says the pirate with the banana bandana.

"Gnmpmnpnp. . ." says the pirate with the dagger in his teeth.

The pirate with the banana bandana throws his knife into the deck. "Well, we've got our own top pirate, isn't that right, boys? Who was it who rammed and looted a Spanish galleon?" he cries.

"Cap'n John the Fierce!" they roar.

"Who was it who single-handedly ate a Portuguese man-of-war jellyfish with custard and chocolate sprinkles?" says the blind fiddle player.

"Cap'n John the Fierce!" they roar.

"And who was it who stole ten thousand false moustaches from the English – right from under their noses?" says Peg Leg Reg.

"CAPTAIN JOHN THE FIERCE!" they roar at the top of their voices.

"Tell me," I interrupt, "who is this Captain John the Fierce? Because he sounds really exciting!"

The pirates all stare at me.

"Why, you're Captain John the Fierce, ya barnacle-brained wassock!" says the pirate with the banana bandana.

"Me?" I laugh. "I mean, of course – me! I'm Captain John the Fierce!"

The pirates all nudge each other and cackle. "You were having a laugh with us," guffaws the pirate with the banana bandana. "Pretending we doesn't know who we is talking about, when we is quite plainly talking about you, Cap'n..."

I try a hearty laugh. The pirate crew laugh even louder. So I take a mouthful of air and give them my best throaty roar.

"Good old Cap'n John the Fierce!" cheer the pirates.

I've never been captain of anything before, not even captain of the school netball team, which I once tried to join to get out of homework.

I jump on a barrel, slap my thigh (they seem to love that sort of stuff) and announce: "I am Captain John the Fierce!" Then I swish my sword around a few times. The four pirates stamp their feet and guffaw.

"And beware he who crosses my path!" I chortle.

I swish my sword one last time. But the sword accidentally flies out of my hand and slices through a net of coconuts, which go rolling all over the deck.

"Our coconuts!" says the pirate with the banana bandana. "Loads of good, tasty

vitamins to ward off nasty diseases like scurvy."

The blind fiddle player starts to play a merry tune and the pirates jig around on the deck.

"Gentleman, raise your jugs to Cap'n John the Fierce, the most feared pirate that ever sailed on the seven seas," says the pirate in the banana bandana.

"And the eighth sea and the ninth sea too," says the blind fiddle player.

"Gnmpmphphph..." says the pirate with the dagger in his teeth.

"Here's to a brutal skirmish where we all get cruelly cut down and lose several limbs!" says the pirate with the banana bandana.

"I'll drink to that," says Peg Leg Reg. He unscrews his leg and pours foamy liquid straight in his gob.

"*You're all going to die! You're all going to*

die!" squawks the parrot. And then he poos all over my shoulder.

This is really brilliant stuff and incredibly believable. I don't know where everyone else from the party is – maybe they're off doing their own adventures and we're all going to meet up later and swap our stories over fizzy drinks and crisps.

I'm so excited I think I'm going to wet myself.

Chapter Four

"I expect you'll want to prepare yourself for the bloody skirmish that is about to follow," says the pirate with the banana bandana, walking with me to what looks like the captain's cabin.

"Oh yes," I chuckle. "I can't wait to get my hands on that Captain Black. Why, I'll kick him in the shin and give him a Chinese burn..."

"And kill him?" says the pirate with the banana bandana.

"You betcha!" I nod.

"And keelhaul him?" he grunts.

"Absolutely. I'll keelhaul him like a good 'un," I reply. "What again, just remind me, is keelhauling?"

"Simple, Captain," he smiles. "You tie a man on to a piece of rope, throw him in the water and drag him under the ship, where the barnacles scrape his belly to bits."

That is a very strange party game! Still, it beats blind man's bluff or stick the tail on the donkey any day of the week.

"I'll man the lookout," says the pirate with the banana bandana. "Will you be wanting your usual pre-skirmish meal, Cap'n?"

"Uh, yes," I reply. "Bring me my usual – and plenty of it!"

I make myself at home in my captain's cabin. It's a brilliant place. There are maps and globes, lots of curly swords on the walls, and best of all … a hammock!

Where is Hector? I hope he's having as much fun as me.

I go to the porthole and pull aside the little curtain.

"AAAAAHHHH!!!"

Who is that mean and wicked pirate staring back at me, a funny three-pointed hat on his head and a natty blue-and-yellow scarf round his throat?

Oh, it's me! It's just my reflection.

"I am Cap'n John the Fierce and I'll have you lot for breakfast," I growl.

I grab a sword off the wall and dance round the cabin, saying things like "Shiver me timbers!" even though I've got no idea what me timbers are or why they're shivering.

I launch myself into the hammock, bounce

out of the netting, splat into the wall and plop on the floor.

"Everything all right, Captain?" says Peg Leg Reg, hobbling through the door with a large pot on a silver tray.

"Oh yes," I reply. "Just trying out the old hammock."

"Nice one, Captain," he cackles. "Anyway, here you go, the captain's lunch!"

Peg Leg Reg pulls the top off the pot.

"Live eels, Cap'n. Your favourite food

before a battle."

Oh dear, the plate is a moving mass of massive worms.

"Put them on the side, Reg. I'll have them later," I groan.

He moves a bit closer and darts his shifty eyes around to make sure no one's listening. "If you don't mind me asking, Captain, but any chance I can see your snarl?"

"My what?" I reply.

"You know, your horribly twisted face," he grunts. "Only, I've followed you into battle many a time, but never got to see your snarl up close..."

"Oh, my snarl? Yes, it's an excellent snarl, one of the best," I chuckle. "Did you know I was snarling champion two years running?"

"Is that a fact?" he replies. "Go on then, just between you and me – show us your snarl."

I twist my face and mouth into a really

mean growl.

Peg Leg Reg stares at me. "That's your snarl?"

Oh dear, I think my snarling powers aren't up to much. I wasn't really snarling champion; I was just trying to play my part.

"You want to know what I do when I give my snarl?" he replies. "I think of the horriblest thought – like I've just come face to face with a disgusting beast of the deep with wild hair and horrible breath!"

So I think of Hayley first thing in the morning.

"Oh, that is a superb snarl!" he says. "They don't call you Cap'n John the Fierce for nothing."

He's right about that. They don't call me

Cap'n John the Fierce at all. They call me John Smith, and some other names I can't tell you about. But this is much better.

I could really get to love being a pirate. I never knew there was so much to it. It's not all about saying "Aaaargh", you know. You get to say "Oooooh-aaaaargh" quite a lot too. And you get to gnarl and gnash your teeth and run round on the deck of the ship swishing your sword. There's a lot of swishing, I can tell you.

It is a brilliant life being a pirate.

Chapter Five

"Captain Black on the horizon," says the pirate with the banana bandana. "Swords at the ready. There's gonna be some skirmishing!"

I leap on to the deck, pull out my telescope and point it at a murky blob coming through the mist.

"That is Captain Black's ship," says Peg Leg Reg. "The *Monstrous Curse*!"

"Good name," I reply. "But it holds no

fear for me, for we sail the meanest ship on the seas..."

I turn and nod at the others, hoping they'll finish my sentence for me, because I haven't got a clue what our ship is called.

"You mean the *Princess Tiffany*?" says the blind fiddle player.

"That's right. A name to strike terror in the heart," I reply, a bit unconvinced by my own answer.

I can see loads of mean rotten types on the deck of the *Monstrous Curse*, waving their swords at us, shouting and jeering. Each pirate looks nastier than the pirate before him.

Standing at the front of the ship is a gobsmackingly horrible-looking pirate with a big black beard down to his toes, a big black eyepatch over his eye and a jungle of wiry black hair worked into funny little pigtails with mini skulls hanging off them.

"I think I see Captain Black..." I mutter to myself.

"What are we gonna do, Cap'n?" says Peg Leg Reg.

Suddenly a cannonball smashes through our sail. This is really, really brilliant stuff. I have no idea where Hector is, but all I'd like to say right now is a massive thank you to his mum and dad for laying on such brilliant entertainment. Well done, Mr and Mrs Siddons!

I lift my sword in the air and holler: "Return fire, men!!!"

The four pirates look at me and scratch their heads.

"What are we gonna return fire with, Captain? We haven't got any cannonballs," says the pirate with the banana bandana.

"Or no cannons neither," says the blind fiddle player.

"*You're going to die! You're going to die!*" squawks the parrot.

Suddenly I get one of my light-bulb moments – or, this being pirate times where there aren't light bulbs, one of my candle moments!

"We'll use coconuts for cannonballs!" I announce.

Another cannonball whistles over our heads, smashes through the rail on the side of the ship and fizzes into the sea.

"We're gonna fight 'em with coconuts?" says the blind fiddle player. "They'll run amok!"

"Gnmphphg..." says the pirate with the dagger in his teeth.

45

"And what are we gonna fire them with?" says Peg Leg Reg.

"Leave that to me," I announce.

I tell the pirates to tie the hammock between the ships masts.

"Thar she goes, Captain," says Peg Leg Reg, "that be good and yare now!"

"That's good work, men," I cry. "Now, before we fire our coconuts, let's get in good and close!"

"Aye aye, Captain," says the pirate with the banana bandana.

The four pirates shuffle up close so we're standing in a little huddle.

"I meant let's get our ship close to the *Monstrous Curse*," I sigh.

We sail the *Princess Tiffany* alongside the *Monstrous Curse*. All the while the cannonballs fly over our heads, smashing into the deck, rolling round at our feet, exploding in the ship's hold.

"They're destroying our beautiful ship, Cap'n," hollers the pirate with the banana bandana. "What are we gonna do?"

"Load up the coconut!" I cry.

The pirates load the coconut in the hammock and pull it back.

"I can't hold it any longer," says Peg Leg Reg. "It's killing my arm!"

"Hurry, Captain," says the pirate with the banana bandana.

"Wait for it … wait for it…" I whisper.

I line up the coconut on the *Monstrous Curse*.

"FIRE!"

The coconut goes zipping out of the hammock and clean over the top of the *Monstrous Curse*, skimming over the ocean like a stone on a pond.

"Did you see that?" I gasp. "One. Two. Three skips. Brilliant!"

The four pirates look at me with long, drawn faces.

"We missed, Cap'n," says the pirate with the banana bandana. "What are we gonna do now?"

The enemy return fire with a heavy blast from the cannons.

"Load up and fire again!" I cry.

The second shell smashes into the ship and splatters coconut everywhere. The pirates hungrily gobble up the coconut, reload their cannons and fire again.

"One more time!" I shout.

"This is madness, Captain, madness," says the pirate with the banana bandana. "They're using live rounds and we're returning fire with tropical fruit!"

"Gnpmphphph..." says the pirate with the dagger in his teeth.

"Good idea, pirate with a dagger in your teeth," I reply. "We'll try just that!"

"What did he say, Captain?" says Peg Leg Reg.

"He says take aim for the main mast holding up the sail," I reply.

"He really said that?" says the blind fiddle player.

"Absolutely," I grin.

We put the final coconut into the hammock.

"OK, boys, let 'em have it!" I yell.

The coconut roars out of the hammock and smashes into the enemy mast. The pirates on the *Monstrous Curse* jeer and boo. Suddenly the mast crashes on to the deck, pulling the sail on to the pirates, trapping them underneath.

"OK, boys," I shout, "swords at the ready. Attack! Attack!"

We swing on to the deck of the *Monstrous Curse* and fly into action.

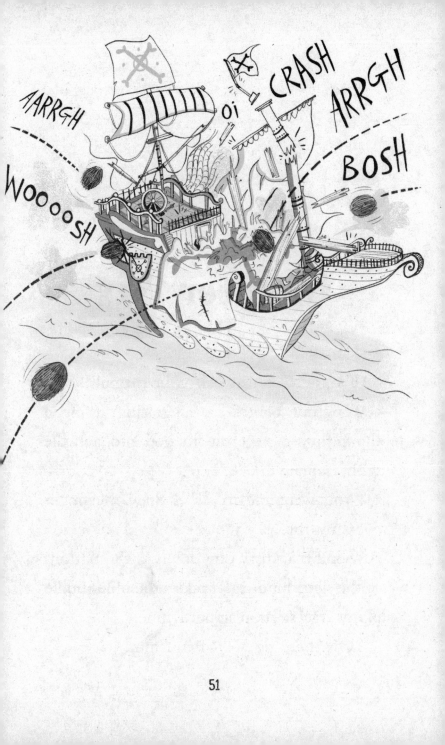

Chapter Six

"All right, Cap'n, work your magic!"

The four pirates are all staring at me. I think they expect me to get into a tussle with Captain Black.

"You want me to...?" I draw my finger over my throat.

"Send that dirty dog down to the bottom of the deep blue sea," cackles the blind fiddle player. He starts playing a tune.

"OK, here goes..." I murmur.

Captain Black looks at me and draws his sword.

"I am Captain Black!" he rages. "I have sailed these seas man and boy. My legend is well known round these parts. I am a fearless pirate with a vicious reputation! Then he leans up really close to me. "What is your name?"

His breath smells of cups of tea and travel sweets.

"I am. . ." I look at the other pirates; they all nod, willing me on. "Why, Cap'n John the Fierce, of course!" I reply in my best firm voice. "I too am expert with a ship!" (If you don't count the time I sank Hayley in a pedalo. . .)

Captain Black starts to laugh, then he coughs and wheezes, bangs his chest with his fist and takes a deep breath.

"Are you sure that is your name?" says Captain Black. "Captain John the Fierce!

Because I don't think you're a real pirate at all!"

Well, I'm not standing for that! After all, my reputation is at stake. My name is everything, even if it is a made-up name and he's completely right.

"Are you calling me a liar, sir?" I growl.

I wink at Captain Black, just to let him know I'm joining in with the fun. I wouldn't want him to think I was actually upset with him.

"I don't like the cut of your jib," says Captain Black.

I've heard them say this in loads of pirate films.

"I HATE the cut of your jib!" I snigger. "It's a really smelly jib. Yuck! Nasty!"

There you go, Captain Black – you don't mess with me!

I look at the others and giggle.

Captain Black draws his sword and points it at my chin.

"I think we should settle this the pirate way, don't you?" he snarls.

"Oh yes, I most certainly do," I reply. I point my sword at his fuzzy, straggly beard.

"Fight! Fight! Fight!" chant the pirates.

So we do.

We have one of those brilliant sword fights where we're both jumping and running all over the ship, attacking and defending, swiping, slicing, slashing, prodding and poking with our swords.

We fight at the front of the ship, we fight at the back of the ship, we fight in the hold, we fight in the crow's nest. It's a full-on MONSTER MASH of a sword fight.

Captain Black lunges at me but I cleverly dance out of the way. He flies over a barrel and lands in a heap.

"Oooh..." he gasps, rubbing his back.

He staggers to his feet, lifts his sword and

rushes at me again. I dive sideways into a pile of nets. Captain Black goes spinning off and smashes into a stack of crates.

"Ooooowwww!" he roars and goes hopping and dancing round the deck with a crab pinching his bottom.

I put my hands on my hips and do my biggest pirate guffaw.

Captain Black sits on a step, takes a big white hanky out of his pocket and mops his brow.

That's when the storm hits.

A great gale rips into the ship. The waves roll as high as houses.

CRACK! goes the thunder.

ZAP! goes the lightning.

GURGLE! goes my belly.

"What's the matter," says Captain Black, "getting seasick?"

"Seasick!" I roar. "I don't know the meaning of the blurghhh. . ."

I hurl a sloppy mess of spaghetti all over my boots.

"Yuck . . . them be eels!" says Peg Leg Reg.

"Ha!" snorts Captain Black. "You haven't got your sea legs!" The ship climbs over the top of a wave and smashes down the other side. "Whereas I, Captain Black, have bwwwaaaaarrrrr..."

Captain Black pukes a massive mound of spaghetti all down his shirt. I dance and duck out of his way, running behind the mast as his sword splinters into the wood, skipping along the rail as he swipes at the rigging, hopping from barrel to barrel as he knocks holes in the deck.

"Had enough yet, Captain Black?" I taunt him.

"No chance," says Captain Black.

Can I just say, for the record, I am one hundred per cent LOVING being a pirate. They ought to teach it at school, because I'd be a straight-A student.

"One minute," says Captain Black. He

puts his hand on his chest and sucks in a few deep breaths, panting like an old man.

"I thought you said this Captain Black was the meanest dog in the land," I whisper to the pirate with the banana bandana.

"What can I say?" he replies. "He hasn't been round our way for several years now."

"Age comes to us all," pants Captain Black. "But no man's brought me down yet..."

He rises unsteadily to his feet. "Have some of this!" he roars.

Captain Black tries to strike out but trips on some rope and falls on to his back, his sword sliding down the deck. "I give up," he gasps and wheezes. "I'm no match for you!"

He pulls some dentures out of his mouth to suck in the sweet, salty air.

I have beaten the feared Captain Black. Honestly, I'm not making it up. This could not go any better.

"Not quite so fast!" says a voice behind me.

When I turn round, the four pirates have muskets raised up.

"Get on your feet, Captain Black!" says the pirate with the banana bandana.

Captain Black climbs to his feet. He struggles to catch his breath as he fumbles around in his pocket.

"He's got a gun!" says Peg Leg Reg.

"Drop it," says the pirate with the banana bandana.

"I haven't got a gun," groans Captain Black. He brings out a hanky and dabs his brow. "I've got a dodgy chest," he wheezes.

"Well, gentlemen, we have defeated the great Captain Black and captured his crew," I boast. "I believe our work here is done."

"Our work is just beginning," says the pirate with the banana bandana. "Captain John the Fierce! Captain Black! I arrest you both in the name of the king."

Chapter Seven

"I am Captain William Maybury of His Majesty's Royal Navy," says the pirate with the banana bandana.

"And I am Charles Kingfisher of His Majesty's Treasury," says Peg Leg Reg.

"I am Sir Peter Potter of the Exchequer," says the blind fiddle player.

"And I'm not a parrot," says the parrot, "but Lance Corporal James Sanderson of the King's Coast Guard!"

The pirate with the dagger in his teeth says, "Gnpnmpmph..."

"You, Captain John the Fierce, otherwise known as John the Nasty, John the Naughty and John the Quite Small but Very Smelly, are under arrest for piracy on the high seas," says Captain Maybury.

"And the low seas and the in-betweeny seas!" I giggle.

"Be silent," says Captain Maybury. "How do you plead?"

Wow, this is a serious twist in the plot. I thought I was the hero but I'm really one of the villains. I suppose the actors at these fancy dress parties have to keep the action lively and interesting, so you can never guess which way the stories going to go. I love it!

"Oh, guilty," I laugh. "Guilty, guilty, guilty. I'm as guilty as they come!"

"In that case," says Lance Corporal James Sanderson, "the sentence is death."

"Excellent," I chuckle. "I fart in the face of death."

"You shall be hanged from the yardarm," says Captain Maybury.

"I don't know what that is, but bring it on," I chuckle.

"Can I just say a word...?" interrupts Captain Black.

"No, you may not, sir!" says Captain Maybury. "This same sentence goes for you too."

Then he turns to me. "Do you have anything to say before sentence is carried out?"

"Yes, I do," I reply. "I would like to say I'm not happy with this whole 'hanged over the yardarm' thingy. It is wrong and totally unfair. We all know pirates have to walk the plank. And this is a perfectly good ship, and that over there is a perfectly excellent plank, and I can see some perfectly nasty sharks swimming round in the waters. So do you think you could grant this special wish? You would be making one little boy very happy indeed..."

"Very well," says Captain Maybury. "Captain Black and Captain John the Fierce will walk the plank. Take them below to await execution."

Lance Corporal James Sanderson begins to lead me off. I turn back to Captain Maybury and smile. "Thank you, this has been a fantastic experience! When do I get my party bag?"

Chapter Eight

"Well, I don't think that could have gone any better," I chuckle as we are locked in the Captain's Cabin. "This is a brilliant party. If only Hector could be here to enjoy it."

"There's something I have to tell you now we're alone," says Captain Black. "I'm not really Captain Black."

"I know that, silly," I chuckle. "You're one of the actors, part of Hector's party."

"I'm not one of the actors," says Captain Black.

Captain Black peels his eyepatch from his eye. Then he tugs his big bushy beard off his chin and throws his big black coat on the floor.

"GRANDDAD!!!"

"Hello, son," he smiles.

"What's going on?" I gasp. "I thought this was Hector's party."

"This isn't a party," says Granddad. "You really are a pirate. I was going to explain everything but I never got a chance. I've come here to make sure you get back safe and sound."

"What are you talking about?" I gulp.

"I was going to tell you all about the John Smith Club," he grins.

"The John Smith Club?" I mumble.

"It's an amazing, incredible, magical thing," says Granddad. "Anyone called John Smith can travel to faraway lands and have crazy adventures."

"Yeah, right," I laugh.

"I'm telling you the truth," says Granddad. "Once upon a time, when I was a young man, I turned myself into Captain Black, and I told my crew I was the nastiest pirate who ever put to sea. Blackbeard, Bluebeard, Redbeard ... I pretended to be meaner than the lot of them. Trouble was, the navy don't like pirates, so I got out in the nick of time."

"What about Dad? Is he a member of this club?"

"He's not called John Smith," says Granddad, "so he doesn't know a thing about it. It's just our little secret – you, me and the other half a million John Smiths on the planet!"

"So this is all real?" I gasp.

"Oh it's real all right," chortles Granddad. He goes to the porthole and looks out. "And that there plank over that there sea with those there sharks swimming in those them waters – well, that's real too."

"Aaaaaaarghhhhh!!!" I scream. "I'm going to walk the plank!"

"Calm down," says Granddad.

"Calm down? I'm too young to get into a wrestling match with an octopus."

"Don't worry," chuckles Granddad. "You were brilliant up on the deck – brave and clever with loads of pluck. Remember what I said. Any fool can pretend to be a pirate. All you have to do is wear a silly hat and coat. But in here, that's where it counts."

Granddad taps his chest with his finger.

"You just have to believe in yourself. Think you can do that?"

"I'll give it a go, Granddad."

"That's the spirit," he chuckles. "Now listen up, because I know a way of getting us out of this tricky situation."

"What's that?"

"All you have to do is say the magic words and you're back home."

"What are the magic words, Granddad?" I gasp.

Captain Maybury opens the door.
Granddad quickly puts his eyepatch and
beard on, then picks his coat up off the floor.

"All right, you two, time you came with us…" orders Captain Maybury.

"What are the magic words, Granddad?" I repeat.

Granddad scratches his head. "Well blow me down, if I haven't gone and forgotten them."

"Gentlemen," says Captain Maybury, "your plank awaits."

Chapter Nine

Me and Granddad shuffle across the deck, step on to the plank and walk to the edge. The endless stretch of sea is dotted with the pointy fins of nasty swirling sharks.

"By order of the king, I sentence you, Captain Black, to death, for acts of piracy on the high seas!" says Captain Maybury.

Granddad nods bravely.

"By order of the king, I sentence you, Captain John the Fierce, to death, for acts

of piracy on the high seas!" repeats Captain Maybury.

I can feel my knees knocking.

"Not so brave now, eh?" laughs Captain Maybury. "As for the rest of your crew −" he gestures at the pirate crew, clapped in irons "− you will be taken to England and thrown in a dirty, damp dungeon for a very long time."

I lean forward and whisper in Granddad's ear.

"What are the magic words, Granddad?"

"They're in here somewhere, son," says Granddad, tapping the side of his head. "The trouble is, so is a lot of other stuff!"

"In that case, it's time for plan B."

"What's plan B?" says Granddad.

"Cross your fingers and hope for the best," I smile. "You ready for one last, crazy roll of the dice?"

"I knew you had it in you, son," says Granddad. "You're going to be one of the great John Smiths!"

"Here we go..."

I begin to jump up and down on the end of the plank.

"By command of the king I order you to stop that bouncing!" says Captain Maybury.

But I don't listen to Captain Maybury. I keep boinging up and down on that plank, getting higher and higher.

"Stop that now," says Captain Maybury. "Stop that or I'll shoot."

He points his musket at me.

"Here goes, Granddad!" I yell.

With one giant bounce I somersault into the air and crash into the stack of crab crates. The crabs shower down on the kings' men, pinching them soundly on their bottoms.

"Gnmphphph..." says Captain William Maybury.

"Grfrfrfrfffff..." says Charles Kingfisher.

"Gmprprrrr..." says Lance Corporal James Sanderson.

"Gnmphph..." says Sir Peter Potter.

"That really hurts," says the pirate with the dagger in his teeth.

I grab the net and toss it over the lot of them, trapping them in a tangle of arms and legs.

"Well done, John; first-class work," laughs Granddad.

We run along the deck of the *Monstrous Curse*, climb on to the rail and leap on to the *Princess Tiffany*.

"This is easy, Granddad," I cheer. "I love this life!"

"You're young; you've got everything ahead of you," says Granddad. "You can have adventures beyond your wildest dreams."

"We both can," I chuckle. "From now on it's going to be you and me together, in the thick of the action..."

The king's men hack their way out of the net.

"Maybe there's life in the old dog yet," chuckles Granddad. "We could be a great team!"

Suddenly we hear a loud explosion.

"Oooh dear," says Granddad, "I think they just blasted a cannonball through the side of our ship!"

"Oh," I mutter, "that's not good is it, Granddad?"

"On a scale of one to ten, I'd say it's an eleven," he frowns.

"What happens now?" I gulp.

"This is the part where we sink to the bottom of the sea," says Granddad.

The ship starts sinking.

"Maybe now would be a good time to remember those magic words, Granddad," I cry.

"You're right, son," says Granddad.

The sea rises over the rail and sloshes round on the deck.

"You'd better hurry, Granddad. My toes are getting wet!"

"Rightio, son," says Granddad.

The deck disappears under the waves.

"The magic words. . ." mutters Granddad. "What are they?"

We shin up the rigging and climb into the crow's nest at the top of the ship, but it's no use. The ship sinks faster and faster, and soon the only thing we're clinging to . . . is each other.

The water rises to our chests and the sharks circle nearer and nearer.

"I think she's about to go down!" says

Granddad.

"The magic words?" I holler.

"Yes, yes … yes…" says Granddad. "Something about pickled beetroot… No, wait … that was the shopping…"

"Hurry, Granddad!"

"Sorry, it's gone out of my brain," he mumbles.

The water bubbles up to our mouths. A seagull swoops down and lands on my head. This is it.

"Oh, Granddad," I cry. "I wish I knew the… Wait a minute, what if it's the same magic words that got me here in the first place?"

"I remember the magic words," says Granddad suddenly. "They're the same magic words that got you here in the first place."

"I just said that, Granddad," I gasp.

"Did you?" chuckles Granddad. "Well, what are you waiting for?"

So we say the words together.

"*Say it long, say it loud – I'm John Smith and I'm proud!*"

Suddenly the ship rises up out of the water, the sun grows massive and the sky starts spinning round faster and faster…

"Hold on tight," says Granddad, "we're going home!"

Chapter Ten

"What did you think of that, John?" says Granddad. "Wasn't that an adventure and a half?"

"That was brilliant, amazing, the best thing EVER!" I laugh. "Though we were nearly eaten alive by sharks!"

"That would have been most unfortunate," giggles Granddad.

We're in the middle of Granddad's bedroom and I'm back in my old clothes. The chest

from under the bed is just where I left it, with the pirate costume right on the top.

"What about Hector's party?" I gulp. "Do you think we've still got time? After all, with my pirate hat and pirate coat, I really look the part."

"And now you can act the part too," laughs Granddad. "If you shake a leg you can still make it."

"You really think so?"

"Time's ticking," says Granddad. "Come on, I'll give you a lift."

I grab the costume and we hop down the stairs.

As I run past the kitchen I stick my head round the door.

"I'm off to Hector's party!" I announce.

Mum wipes her hands down on a tea towel and gives me a peck on the cheek. "Have a nice time, love," she smiles.

"Don't do anything I wouldn't do," says Dad from behind the newspaper.

"I'll be back later on," I cheer.

"Aye aye, Cap'n John the Boring," says Hayley.

Granddad wheels his old boneshaker tandem out of the garage. "This was a present from Queen Victoria," he laughs, levering himself on to the front seat. "We used to go riding round Buckingham Palace together!"

"That's a joke, right, Granddad?" I chuckle.

"You'll just have to find out for yourself," winks Granddad. "Now you know about the John Smith Club, you can be a pirate, a spaceman, a knight in shining armour, a cowboy ... you can be whatever you want to be. And don't you ever let anyone tell you otherwise. Like I say, just because you've got a boring name doesn't mean you're boring or that you've got a boring life..."

"This is going to be a blast, Granddad!" I laugh, climbing into the saddle behind him.

"Come on, let's get you to Hector's party!" says Granddad.

"You'll love Hector," I chuckle. "He's such really brilliant fun!"

"I'll bet he's not as much fun as you, John," smiles Granddad. "John Smith is boring? Not on your nelly!"

ACKNOWLEDGEMENTS

A mahousive, ginormous thank you to my small army of readers (sorry, my army of small readers) Lucien and Manon Abbott, Emma Beart, Tom Francis, Louis Johnson, Angus Macdonald, Jago McGuinness, Thomas Norrey, Daisy Smith and Jacob Thornhill. To the wonderful Zoe Duncan for kicking it all off. To my friends and family whose ears I bent regularly, Will Brenton, Ian Pike and Lottie Wake. My fantastic agent Gemma and the amazing folk at Scholastic especially the fabulous Rachel Phillipps and of course my brilliant editor Helen Thomas who indulged her childishly enthusiastic author with grace and calm. And finally the incredibly talented Lil for the superb pictures.

Everyone is chanting my name...

"John Smith! John Smith! John Smith!"

I'm riding into a castle on a huge black horse. The bells in the tower are ringing out; the crowds are cheering.

Someone shouts out, "John Smith has come to save us!"

Someone else shouts out, "All hail John Smith!"

And then someone says, "He is the greatest

name in the land!"

What can I say? I like the sound of this! I give the crowd a big wave and they all cheer again.

"You are most popular, sire!" says a boy who's holding my horse as he leads me into the courtyard. "John Smith is such an amazing and wonderful name. I've never heard anything like it."

"It's true it is a very rare name," I reply. "Down my way I'm one of a kind."

"I am Oswald Periwinkle," says the boy. "I know what you're thinking. You're thinking, what a very common name. When I asked my father why he called me Oswald Periwinkle, he said—"

"Because with a name like that, no one will ever make fun of you?" I interrupt.

Oswald looks at me and gasps. "You can read my mind, John Smith. It's true what they say — you are touched by greatness!"

Oswald holds his hand out to help me off the horse.

"Come with me. The Queen is waiting in her castle." He pats me on the shoulder and smiles. "You can call me Ossie."

I follow Ossie into the castle, through a massive hall with pictures of old kings and queens on the walls and past the heralds blowing their trumpets.

A messenger shouts out, "All kneel for Her Majesty, the Queen!"

At the top of the hall the Queen sits on a shiny gold throne wearing a shiny gold crown.

I kneel before her.

Standing next to the Queen is a really scary man with an axe who looks just like my headmaster. "Watch out for him," whispers

Ossie. "That's the Queen's executioner, Woodworm!"

The Queen rises to her feet and looks at me. Everyone listens very closely.

"John Smith, your name is legend around these parts. And such an unusual name..." says the Queen.

The crowd all nod their heads.

"You are probably wondering why we have sent for you."

"Speak, Your Queenliness," I reply.

"We have a big problem," says the Queen. "Ivan the Horrible is going to wreak havoc on our castle, causing much mayhem and misery. This is why we have sent for you, John Smith! We want you to do battle with Ivan the Horrible and we really want you to try your hardest to KILL him!"

"They don't call me John Smith for nothing, Your Majesty!" I reply. "I'll take care of your little problem."

"Three cheers for John Smith!" someone shouts out.

And everyone cheers, including the horses.

The Queen slumps in her throne and scratches her cheek. "Haven't I seen you somewhere before?" she says.

"Oh no, Your Majesty, there is only one of me!" I laugh. Which of course is a completely enormous fib; there are millions of me!

"Very well, then. Eat, drink and be merry," she chuckles. "For very soon you will probably be dead."

TO BE CONTINUED...

Other

NOT
BORING!

adventures from

John Smith

Johnny Smith is an experienced animation and live-action screenwriter. As one half of Sprackling and Smith, the comedy screenwriting team, he sold numerous original feature film scripts here and in Hollywood, including Disney's box office hit GNOMEO & JULIET. He lives in London with his wife and children.